Abracadabra!

Boo! Ghosts
in the School!

Abracadabra!

Boo! Ghosts in the School!

By Peter Lerangis
Illustrated by Jim Talbot

A
LITTLE APPLE
PAPERBACK

SCHOLASTIC INC.

New York   Toronto   London   Auckland   Sydney
Mexico City   New Delhi   Hong Kong   Buenos Aires

For Tina, Nick, and Joe,
the magic in my life.

ISBN 0-439-22231-1

12 11 10 9 8 7 6 5 4 3 2 1   1 2 3 4 5 6/0

Printed in the U.S.A.
First Scholastic printing, October 2001

Contents

Contents

1

One-eyed Pete

"He's scary," said Noah Frimmel.

"He's wooden," noted Quincy Norton.

"He's cute," said Selena Cruz.

"He's history!" Jessica Frimmel had had enough. Everybody was fussing over Wilbur Doodle. He was going to ruin the whole day. "Wilbur cannot come to our meeting."

Wilbur Doodle's eyes rolled and his

mouth clacked. *"Don't be cruel! Keep me in school!"*

Wilbur was made of wood. His hair was plastic and black. On each cheek he had five dime-sized freckles, painted by Max Bleeker. He spoke only in rhymes, except when Max couldn't think of any. He wore Max's old jeans, red shirt, and white baby shoes. Everyone called him a dummy, but Max didn't like that.

"*He*'s not talking," said Noah. "*You* are, Max."

"I'm throwing my voice," Max replied. "Could you see my lips move? I'm trying to say *m*'s and *b*'s and *p*'s without moving my lips. But they all sound like *v*'s."

"We noticed," said Quincy. His head was tilted a little, because it was hard to see through his dusty glasses. Quincy was the smartest fourth grader at Rebus Elementary

School. He remembered names. He remembered dates. He remembered anything he had ever seen on a sheet of paper. But nobody ever wrote down "Tie your shoes," or "Clean your glasses," so sometimes, he didn't.

Quincy, Jessica, Max, and Selena were members of the Abracadabra Club. On the day Wilbur Doodle came to school, the club was meeting for its first time ever. The meeting was going to start right after the final bell. Jessica couldn't wait. She wanted everything to be Totally Perfect.

But Wilbur was Totally Annoying.

"Max," Jessica said. "If you bring Wilbur to our meeting, you're just going to play with him. We won't get anything done —"

"Okay, kids, show's over!" shouted Mr. Flint, the computer teacher. "Time to go to class!"

Mr. Flint had a thick red beard. It moved like a furry animal when he talked. He loved to joke around, and he always moved fast fast fast. But today he was leaning on a cane.

"Hey, what happened to your leg?" asked Andrew Flingus.

Mr. Flint lowered his voice. "One-eyed Pete did this to me."

Andrew scratched his head. A tiny spitball fell out. It had been in his hair for two days. Andrew was the most awful kid in the fourth grade. "*Who?*" he asked.

"One-eyed Pete, the ghost of Rebus," said Mr. Flint quietly. "He lives in the auditorium. And he *hates* it when grown-ups use the stage. Well, the Rebus Theater Group is putting on a new play in our auditorium. Last night I was here helping them. I was still at school after everybody had gone home. That's when I heard a noise in the hallway. A moan."

5

Noah squeezed Jessica's hand — hard.

"I tried to run," Mr. Flint went on, "and *wham*! He jumped out of the wall and grabbed my leg!"

"Cool!" said Andrew.

Most of the other kids giggled and pretended to be afraid. They all knew Mr. Flint was joking. But not Noah. He was only six years old, and lately he was afraid of *everything*.

"It's just a story," Jessica whispered.

"But Mom and Dad are in that show!" Noah said.

"Only one other thing gets One-eyed Pete angry," Mr. Flint said. "When kids don't go to their classes in the morning! Now go, before he finds you here!"

"Eek!" screamed Andrew, in a fake, high voice. His sneakers squished as he ran away.

Everyone began walking to class. But

Noah wouldn't let go of Jessica's hand. "Walk with me?" he asked.

"Noah," Jessica said with a sigh, "there is no One-eyed Pete."

"Well, there *was*," Quincy corrected her. "I read about him. He was an actor who lived in the 1800s. He lost his eye in a sword fight in a play. While visiting Rebus, he was thrown in jail for a crime he didn't do. He died there. The legend says his ghost is still trapped in the jailhouse."

"Good!" Noah said. "If he's in jail, that means he *couldn't* be here!"

"Not exactly." Quincy smiled and pointed to a faded brass sign on the wall:

> REBUS ELEMENTARY SCHOOL
>
> 1967
>
> FORMERLY THE HISTORIC
>
> REBUS PRISON

"We go to school in a *jail*?" Selena asked.

"It *used* to be a jail," Quincy said. "One-eyed Pete's cage was where the auditorium is. Every year Pete haunts the Rebus Theater Group's play. See, he doesn't know he's dead. He wants to be in the play."

Max put a hand over Wilbur's right eye. *"Just call me One-eyed Wilbur the ghost! Begone, or you're toast! Ah-ha-ha-ha!"*

Noah burst into tears. "STOP!"

BRRRINNNGG! went the school bell.

Jessica pulled Noah away from Max. She quickly walked him to his class.

"Don't let Max and Quincy scare you," she said, stopping outside the doorway. "One-eyed Pete is a tall tale. Tall tales aren't true, okay?"

Noah nodded. As he turned to go inside, Jessica raced down the hall to Room 104.

She could see Max walking into his class-room, Room 110.

Suddenly, a moan, low and soft, made Jessica spin around.

She began to feel very cold. Her mouth went dry.

"Max?" she called out. "Stop trying to throw your voice! It's not funny."

But Max didn't answer. He was already in class.

The moan faded into nothing. It seemed to be coming from the walls themselves.

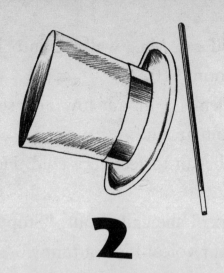

2

Numa, Scribe, and the Main Brain

"Dancing in the darrrrrk," sang Mr. Skupa, the janitor, in a creaky voice. He danced with his broom as he swept an old basement storage room.

Selena tried not to laugh. Mr. Skupa was so corny. Carefully she taped a big sign onto the door.

OFFICIAL, PERMANENT
ABRACADABRA
CLUBHOUSE!
Sign made by Selena Cruz

As she stepped back to admire her sign, Selena brushed her hair. Hairbrushing was her favorite hobby, along with artwork, shopping, and butting into other people's business.

"Looks cool!" Quincy said.

"It will look better when the room is clean," Selena said, gazing at the swirls of dust around Mr. Skupa's broom.

Jessica and Max were helping unpack boxes full of magic tricks. The boxes belonged to Stanley Beamish, Semi-famous Wild West Magician. Jessica could still hardly believe that he was their new teacher — *plus* the head of the Abracadabra Club.

Mr. Beamish had a shiny head and a pointy black beard. He spoke in a deep voice. "A new room for our club," he said, "and it seems we have a new mystery — voices in the hallway. Jessica, you're not the only one who's heard funny noises. At least three other kids said they heard the ghost, too."

"The noise sounded like Max to me," Jessica said.

"Maybe it was my tummy," Max said. "I had ice cream for breakfast."

"Whatever," Selena said. "It's something normal, I'm sure, not One-eyed Pete. That's just a silly old story."

"Ain't he sweeeet…One-eyed Peeeete…" sang Mr. Skupa, sweeping up the last dust ball into a pile by the door. "Welcome to

12

your new home, gentlemen and ladies! For my last trick, I shall make this pile of dust disappear."

"Wait, I'll help you!" Quincy suddenly said. He grabbed the dustpan by its handle, which was about three feet long. "Wow, this is heavier than it looks. Guess I'm going to have to use the think system, Mr. Skupa."

Mr. Skupa scratched his head. "The what?"

"It goes like this. You close your eyes and think . . . really hard." Quincy closed his eyes. He lifted the dust pan. His right arm began to shake. He grabbed his right wrist with his left hand. Now both arms were shaking. "Okay . . . here goes . . ."

Slowly Quincy opened his right fist, the one that was holding the handle. Thumb . . . index finger . . . middle . . . Soon his hand was stretched out — but the dustpan did not

drop. The handle was still attached to the palm of his hand!

Quincy set the dustpan on the floor next to Mr. Skupa. "There!" he said. "That made it much easier."

"Heee-hee-hee!" Mr. Skupa laughed and clapped his hands. "I'll be a monkey's uncle! How did you do that?"

"A magician never reveals his tricks!" Mr. Beamish reminded him.

"Well, may your opening night of the Abracadabra Club be fantastic. As they say in the theater . . . break a leg!" Mr. Skupa scooped up the dust and backed out of the room.

Selena turned to Mr. Beamish. "Why did he say that?"

"It's an old expression," Mr. Beamish explained. "Actors say it all the time. If you wish for something bad, something good happens."

"I hope we're attacked by mice and bugs and worms!" Max said. "And then it starts to snow, only the snow is really chunks of dead fish, and —"

"Uh, thanks, Max," Mr. Beamish said. "Ahem. I call this meeting to order."

Quincy opened a brand-new notebook with the words OFFICIAL ABRACADABRA CLUB RECORDS written on the cover. He took out a pen and began writing. "Let's see . . . three twenty-one P.M. . . . first official meeting begins."

"I vote for Quincy to be our secretary," Selena said. "He never stops writing."

Quincy nodded. "Yes, but call me Scribe, not secretary," Quincy said. "Scribe means writer."

"All in favor of Quincy as official scribe, say aye!" Mr. Beamish called out.

"AYE!" shouted Jessica, Max, and Selena.

Max held up Wilbur Doodle. *"The choice for president is plain — Jessica Frimmel is our main brain! Vote for her or it'll be a pain! All in flavor?"*

"The word is *favor*," Quincy said.

"And you moved your lips," added Selena.

"Ay-yi-yi, you have to say aye!" said Wilbur.

"AYE!" said Selena, Quincy, and Max.

"Yyyyyyyes!" said Jessica. "I mean, thanks! What about Max? He should be something."

Mr. Beamish was scratching his chin. "Max is definitely a club Numa."

"What's that?" Max asked.

"Whatever you want it to be," Mr. Beamish said.

"Numa means . . . head wizard! I'm going to be the head wizard," Max exclaimed. "Wow . . . thanks!"

The rest of the meeting raced by. Selena was chosen to be Club Designer. Tuesdays and Fridays, 3:30 to 4:30, were chosen as meeting times. And Quincy started two new notebooks: a Mystery Log and a List of New Tricks.

The hour was almost over when Jessica remembered one of the most important things. "Oh! I almost forgot. We have to talk about how to get new members."

Mr. Beamish nodded. "This is an official club now, so anyone in the school can join."

"Even Andrew Flingus?" Selena cried out. "Ugh."

"We'll just ask One-eyed Pete to scare him away," said Max.

"You four will be the leaders of the group," Mr. Beamish said. "You'll have fun teaching the others magic. Tomorrow we can post a sign-up sheet."

Selena's eyes brightened. "What if we put on a show to get new members? To show people what we do."

"A show, starring me! Wilbur — wheeee!" said Wilbur.

"Seriously," Selena said. "I could do costumes and hair —"

"I could write the script," Quincy said.

"I'll ask Mr. McElroy for permission to use the auditorium," Mr. Beamish said.

Everyone began talking at once — with a million suggestions.

Jessica smiled. The Abracadabra Club was in business!

3

Commotion in the Cafeteria

"Friday?" Selena nearly dropped her turkey sandwich on the lunchroom floor. "How can we do our magic show on Friday? It's already Wednesday!"

"That was the only day Mr. Beamish could get the auditorium," Max explained.

Jessica's mind was spinning. She hadn't even touched her lunch. This show was a big problem. She wished Quincy didn't have chess club today during lunch. He always had good ideas for problems like this.

"I call an emergency meeting after school today," Jessica said. "We need to practice right away."

"We should at least start to *tell* people about the show," Selena said.

Max stood up from the table, whirling his cape through the air. "LADIEEES AND GENTLEMEN! THIS FRIDAY, THE WORLD-FAMOUS ABRACADABRA CLUB PROUDLY PRESENTS ITS FIRST MAGIC SHOE!"

"Show," Jessica whispered. Max always mixed up his words when a crowd was watching.

"ER, YES . . . *SHOW*. TRICKS TO FOOL YOUR EYE AND TICKLE YOUR FUNNY BONE — AND A SPECIAL GUEST!"

"Yeah, One-eyed Pete!" Andrew Flingus called out. He covered his eye with a hamburger bun and began stumbling around the room. "I'm waaaaaiting for you all in the theater! Har har har!"

At the next table, Erica Landers and her snobby friends started to giggle. "Hey, Selena," Erica called out. "You are *not* in this dumb club, are you?"

Jessica slowly turned, smiling sweetly. "Max," she said. "Let's give everyone an idea of our show. Why don't we cut Erica in half?"

Erica burst out laughing. "Sure, Jessica. Where's your toy saw?"

"Not with a saw . . . with these." Jessica reached into her backpack and pulled out two long ropes. "It's easy. We just pull one of them right through your belly."

Erica stopped laughing.

"Do it!" someone shouted from the back of the cafeteria.

"Scared?" Jessica asked.

"No way!" Erica said. She turned toward Mr. Snodgrass, the teacher in charge. "It's just — um, you're not allowed to do that in the cafeteria! Right, Mr. Snodgrass?"

Mr. Snodgrass shrugged. "It would be interesting."

"DO IT! DO IT! DO IT!" a chant went up.

Erica's friends pushed her toward Jessica.

"Max and I will hold both of these ropes behind Erica's back," Jessica announced. "Then, *abracadabra* — we will pull the ropes right through her." She sighed. "We'll try not to rip up your shirt. It's really nice."

"Th-th-thanks," Erica said.

The lunchroom was silent. Max and Jessica stood on either side of Erica. They slowly moved apart so that the ropes were stretched tightly behind her. Jessica gave one end of her rope to Max. He gave one to her.

They tied a square knot in front of Erica's body, and pulled. Erica was trapped.

"One . . ."

"This is a joke, right?" Erica asked. She was starting to look really scared.

"Two . . ."

Max closed his eyes.

"Three!"

Jessica pulled. Max pulled. Erica screamed!

Twwwwippp!

Suddenly, the ropes were in front of Erica. It looked as though they had passed right through her.

Erica's friends started to laugh. One by one, everybody in the lunchroom started clapping.

Shaking, Erica went back to her chair and sat down. She felt her tummy, to be sure she was in one piece.

Selena smiled at Jessica. "Thanks."

"That's just a taste of what you'll see on Friday!" Jessica announced. "I know a lot of you will want to join us —"

"And don't forget our special guest!" said Max, quickly dropping the rope and picking up Wilbur. *"Not One-eyed Pete — he is a pest. But Wilbur Doodle — he's the best!"*

"Not now, Max," Jessica hissed.

"Boo!" shouted Andrew Flingus's friend Luke Larch. "Max, you are the world's worst ventrickle — ventrick — villtrenk — dummy-talker-guy I ever saw!"

"Ventriloquist," Max said.

"Um, anyway," Jessica went on, "we've started a new group called the Abracadabra Club —"

"Hey, Max," shouted a voice from the back. "Can you throw your voice into the toilet?"

Now everyone was laughing. "Please!" Jessica shouted. This was so embarrassing.

"Oh, great," Selena said. "We were doing so well until Wilbur had to open his big mouth, Max!"

"Wilbur Doodle's boring!" shouted Luke. "We want One-eyed Pete! We want One-eyed Pete!"

"There's no such thing!" Selena replied.

Suddenly, from the walls of the lunchroom came a long, deep call:

"BOOOOOOO-AH-HA-HA-HA-HA!"

4

Thumps-a-lot

"Aaaagh!" screamed Mr. Snodgrass.

Jessica nearly jumped to the ceiling. Selena dropped her hairbrush, which she had just started to use.

The whole cafeteria turned toward the sound. It was coming from near the kitchen entrance. No one made a move.

"OhhhhHHHHHH!" the voice moaned.

"Time to go," Max squeaked, picking up Wilbur.

But Jessica crept slowly toward the kitchen. Something about the voice sounded familiar.

"Jessica, what are you doing?" Selena said.

Jessica ignored her. She leaned against the wall by the kitchen doorway.

"HELLLLLP MEEEE!" moaned the voice.

Jessica raced in the door. "Come out right now!"

She grabbed Andrew Flingus by the arm and pulled him into the cafeteria. He was holding a paper-towel tube. Grinning, he held it to his mouth and shouted, *"HAR! HAR! HAR!"*

"Flingus," Mr. Snodgrass said, "I would like to have a word with you."

Andrew was in trouble. Big trouble.
Which was just fine with Jessica.

Every Wednesday during lunch, Quincy
Norton had chess club. The club met in the
hallway behind the stage. Quincy loved chess,
but he hated this time of year. This was when
the Rebus Theater Group put on its winter
play. They didn't have their own stage, so they
used the elementary school's. And they always stored their costumes in the chess club
room. The costumes smelled like mothballs.
Quincy was allergic to mothballs.
"Chhhhheckmate!" Quincy said, sneez-
ing in the middle of the word. As usual, he
had won his game.
"Time's almost up," said Ms. Romanov,
the chess club teacher. "Quincy, you may
leave early and go back to the lunchroom if
you're uncomfortable."

"Thank you-*chooooo*!" Quincy sneezed.

Picking up his notepad and backpack, he ran into the hallway. It was empty and dark there. But the air was clear, and Quincy could breathe again. He quickly made a note in his pad:

LUNCHTIME CHESS PRACTICE	
WINS ⵌ ⵌ ⵌ ⵌ ⵌ ⵌ ⵌ ⵌ ⵌ ⵌ |||	LOSSES

He began heading down the hall, toward the cafeteria. The ceiling lights made a low, buzzing noise.

That was when he heard the moan. And the voice.

It was soft, like the sound of a TV in another room. He couldn't tell what it was saying. But he could just make out one word. "Friday."

Then he heard a laugh. Deep and loud. *HRUMMMMMMMM!*

Quincy jumped at the noise. He spun around. His glasses flew off and fell to the floor. Quincy could barely see without his glasses.

But he could hear the sound of footsteps.

Thump . . . thump . . . thump . . .

Someone — or some*thing* — was coming closer. Quincy tried to see it. But the hallway was a blur of green paint and yellow tile. Except for something that glowed. Something inside one of the rooms.

Quincy made his eyes narrow. The glow

became clear. It was a pirate. A grinning pirate with a patch over one eye and a long sword!

"Yeeps," Quincy squeaked.

He picked up his glasses and ran all the way to the lunchroom. He nearly knocked Jessica over on her way out.

"I heard him!" Quincy blurted out. "By the chess club."

"Who?" Max asked. "One-eyed Pete?"

"No!" Quincy said. "I mean, yes! I mean, I heard a hum and then a thumping noise, like a ghost. And I saw a pirate, who floated like a ghost. Except I don't believe in ghosts. Okay. Okay. I'm calm. I am going to log this into our files right now. But right after school, we have to investigate!"

"But we need to have a meeting to talk about the magic show. It's on Friday —" Jessica began to protest.

"We are a magic and *mystery* club,"

Quincy said. "This is a big mystery. We need to solve it. Meet me outside of Room 104."

After school, Quincy led Jessica, Max, and Selena to the hallway that ran behind the stage.

"We're here — now where's the pirate?" asked Max.

"Let's check all the rooms," Quincy said.

They quietly walked down the hall, trying each door. The first two were locked tight. The third opened into a room full of lights. There were red, blue, and green lights, lights on poles, lights attached to wooden planks. The fourth room was full of props — fake telephones and TVs, tables, chairs, dressers, plastic plants, and a rubber chicken.

"No wonder they have to store the costumes in the chess club room," Jessica said. "The rest of these rooms are a mess."

"Who's putting on this play?" Selena asked.

"The Rebus Theater Group," Jessica told her. "My parents are in it."

"Maybe they've seen One-eyed Pete!" Max said.

"They joked about him," Jessica replied. "They said he moves things around and made some noises. But Noah got scared, so they stopped making jokes. But those *were* jokes. One-eyed Pete is not real."

"Ssshhh!" Quincy said. He pointed to a door at the end of the hall. It was wide open. Inside, the room was pitch-black except for a tiny red light.

"I'm not going in there," Selena whispered.

"Fine," Jessica said. "I will." She tiptoed

to the dark room and reached inside. She felt along the wall and found a light switch. With a quick flick, she pushed it up.

HRUMMMMMMMMM . . .

"Yeeaaaaaggghh!" Jessica jumped away. She crashed into Max, then bounced back into the room.

She landed on a clump of wires, near a table leg. The noise was just above her.

It was a computer. A big, old one. It sat on a long table with lots of electronic equipment — monitors, computers, keyboards, and radios.

"What is this place?" Jessica asked.

Quincy shrugged. "I guess it's where old school equipment goes to die."

"Let's get out of here," Selena said, "before someone finds us."

"Look!" Quincy cried out. He was staring at the computer screen. A glowing pirate stared back. Above the pirate were the words GHOSTS, VAMPIRES, PIRATES, AND OTHER LEGENDARY CREATURES. "This is what I saw at lunchtime."

Selena leaned forward for a look. "You must have lost your appetite. It's scary."

"It's only a picture," Quincy said.

"Yeah? Well, the picture must have dropped something." Max bent down and picked something up off the floor.

A black eye patch.

Thump . . . thump . . . thump . . .

They all froze. A sound was coming from the hallway.

"Quick!" Jessica said. "Hide!"

5

Moaning, Noon, and Night

Quincy squatted behind a small card-board box. Max covered his face with his cape. Jessica tried to squeeze behind a TV stand, but it was too close to the wall.

"We're toast," Selena said.

"Quick, where's one place a ghost would never look?" Max asked.

"The bathroom?" Quincy said.

"You're a genius!" Jessica ran to the

back of the room and pushed aside a coat-rack. Behind it was a door that opened to an old washroom. "In here!"

Thump . . . thump . . . THUMP . . . THUMP . . . The noise was getting closer.

Max, Quincy, and Selena piled inside. Quietly, Jessica stepped in and pulled the door shut. From the room came a crash. A scraping noise. A growl.

Jessica pressed her ear to the door. "He's in there!" she whispered.

Wilbur's wooden teeth were clacking.

"Stop shaking, Max!" Jessica whispered.

"Skupa, Skupa, Skupa . . ." a voice muttered from inside the room.

It was Mr. Flint's voice.

The hrrummming noise stopped, but the thumping started again. It became softer and softer until it faded away.

Jessica pushed the bathroom door open. "It was Mr. Flint fixing the computer, that's all."

"Why was he talking about Mr. Skupa?" Quincy asked.

"Good question," Selena said.

"Let's get out of here," Jessica said, heading for the hallway. "It's way too creepy."

They ran out of the room and through the hall.

At the top of the basement stairs, Noah was waiting. His arms were folded across his chest. "I want to go home."

"You have the after-school program today," Jessica replied. "Mom and Dad aren't home — and I'm having a meeting!"

She took Noah by the arm and marched him to the auditorium. His eyes were wide with fear. "But I heard more noises, Jessica.

Other kids heard them, too! There really *is* a ghost."

"You're all imagining things. One-eyed Pete is made up," Jessica said, opening the auditorium door and gently pushing Noah inside. As she ran back to the basement stairs, she murmured under her breath, "At least I think he is."

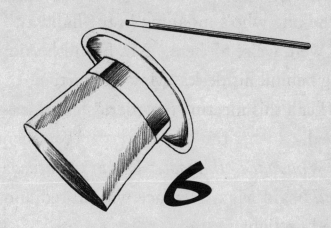

6

171 Minutes

"First you *relax* your lips," Mr. Beamish said. "You keep a big space in the back of your throat. Then *look* where you're trying to throw your voice . . ."

A tiny voice seemed to pipe up from the back of the room. *"Hello, there!"*

"Wow, Mr. Beamish is good," Jessica said.

"*Real* good," Selena whispered. "Maybe he's the one who's moaning in the hallway."

"Well, we're all here," Mr. Beamish said, sitting behind his desk. "May we start?"

"I call this meeting to order!" Jessica exclaimed.

"*Whaaaat's thaaaat, I can't heeeear yooou!*" said Max. His face was all red and twisted up tight.

"Max," Selena said, "are you getting sick?"

"No, I'm throwing my voice!" Max said with a big grin. "The real way. Didn't you hear it coming from the other side of the room?"

Mr. Beamish smiled. "You're doing fine, Max. Perhaps you can use Wilbur onstage during Friday's show."

"But what tricks are we going to do?" Selena asked.

"I know a million card tricks!" Quincy said.

"How about levitation — you know, people floating in the air?" Jessica asked. "You can see that from the back row. Everybody would love it."

"The most important things," Selena said, "are scenery and costumes. If we look like magicians, people will like us — even if our tricks stink. My mom has this black material. I see us in long, flowing robes — oh, and maybe a red sash. . . ."

"Let's get started," Mr. Beamish said. "You already know lots of tricks. We'll practice today and tomorrow. On Friday we can have a dress rehearsal before classes."

Quincy was scribbling in his pad. "We're going to need at least ten tricks."

"No," said Max, rubbing his hands together. "A hundred!"

By 4:30, the club had picked one trick. Just one.

Jessica couldn't believe it. At this rate, the show would be ready in two months!

That night, she didn't eat a thing for dinner. She could barely get any homework done. She tossed and turned in her sleep. She had bad dreams.

And to make things worse, Noah whined all through breakfast the next morning.

"This is the worst day of my life!" Jessica said as they left for school. "Can't you stop complaining?"

"All you think about is your dumb show," Noah said.

"And all you think about is a dumb make-believe ghost!" Jessica replied.

As usual, Quincy was waiting for them

at the corner. He was writing in his notepad. "Jessica, we have nine magic tricks to go. It takes us an average of nineteen minutes to practice a trick —"

"Nineteen? How do you know?" Jessica asked.

"I look at my watch," Quincy replied. "Now, for nine tricks we need 171 minutes. We can practice during recess and lunch. Then we can meet for two hours after school. That will give us . . ." Quincy tapped on a calculator clipped to his pad. "About 210 minutes. That's enough time — with thirty-nine minutes to spare!"

"Quincy?" Noah said. "Are you really a computer?"

Jessica made Quincy repeat the plan. Three times. They took a shortcut around the duck pond, so no one would bother them.

The shortcut led them to the school parking lot. As they walked among the cars, Jessica felt much better.

Quincy was right. They could do it.

She watched Noah run off with his friends. Ms. Romanov was getting out of her car, and Quincy stopped to talk.

Jessica headed into school by herself. Most of the kids were in the front lobby, so the back hallway was nice and quiet.

Too quiet.

Jessica tried to whistle, but no sound came out. She walked faster.

"Myaaahhh! They'll seeee meeee . . ."

Suddenly, a voice came from nowhere. And everywhere. Jessica stopped. "H-hello?" she squeaked.

"They'll see me, they will! On Friday, I'll make them see me! And THEN they'll be sorry!"

7

Stage Fright

"But One-eyed Pete *was* there!" Noah whined. "Yesterday, at after-school! Everyone heard him. He moaned, like this: '*Oooh . . . myaaah-myaaah-myaaah . . .*'"

"'Myaaah?'" asked Jessica's dad as he left the kitchen. "I thought ghosts said boo."

Jessica couldn't eat her eggs. She could barely sit down. It was Friday, the day of the magic show, and her mind was all tangled.

Quincy's plan had worked. The Abracadabra Club had practiced nine tricks on Thursday. But all day, Jessica had felt weird.

She hadn't told anyone about the voice she heard before school. There just hadn't been enough time. But at least ten other kids had claimed to hear it.

There was no question. It had to be real.

Don't think about it, Jessica told herself. *Think of the show. Only the show.*

"Can we go now?" she asked. "We have to practice our magic show onstage before school —"

Noah's face turned white. "You can't go on the stage today! He'll get you!"

"Noah, will you stop!"

"That's what he said. *'Friday's the daaaaay . . . I'll get them on Fridaaaaay!'* I heard him."

"Noah Frimmel, if you do not put your shoes on right this minute," Jessica said, "I will drag you to school in your socks!"

Noah stomped across the kitchen and put on his shoes. "Okay, but I'm not going into that auditorium!"

The stage was very cold that morning. Much colder than Jessica remembered it. She kept telling herself, *It's always cold in the morning. This has nothing to do with a ghost in the school.* This was the club's final practice. She had to concentrate.

Selena was busy sweeping the stage. "The grown-ups left a big mess last night after their rehearsal," she complained. "They're worse than kids!"

"I wonder if they hear the voices, too," Jessica said.

Selena folded her arms and looked at Jessica. "Hear *my* voice, Jessica — you have to stop thinking about this!"

"Okay, five minutes to go before school starts!" Mr. Beamish called out. "Let's practice the big one — the Disappearing Quincy Trick!"

Jessica ran to the curtain ropes. The curtains had to be closed for this trick. She pulled, leaving only a little gap in the center, just wide enough for one person to pass through. Then she tiptoed to the gap and hid just inside.

Quincy was in front of the curtain, where the audience would see him. "*Psssst!* Jessica? Are you ready?"

"Yup!"

In front of the curtain, Max and Quincy held up a big, thick blanket. They stretched it apart so the blanket was as tight as a sail.

They made sure the bottom edge touched the floor, and the top edge was high above their heads.

Quincy stepped behind the sheet, still holding it up. From the audience, it would look as if Quincy were rolling himself up into a mummy. Afterward, Max would say a magic word and quickly unroll Quincy — only it wouldn't be Quincy anymore. He'd transform into Jessica!

The trick was, Jessica had to step through the curtain and switch places with Quincy — now, before the wrapping started.

"Friday . . . I'll get them all on Friday!"

The voice! Jessica could hear the voice. It was soft and far away. But where? Where was it?

"Quickly!" Quincy hissed, holding the edge of the sheet above his head.

Jessica grabbed it and took his place. As

he slipped backstage through the curtain, she slowly rolled herself up.

The blanket was warm. Too warm. She couldn't see a thing.

Trapped, she thought. *I am trapped.*

"AND NOW, FLEECE YOUR EYES ON THE NEW QUINCY!" Max said.

"*Feast* your eyes!" Quincy called from backstage.

"ABRACADABRA . . . ZOOT . . . FEEZBORGEN!" Max shouted.

He pulled — hard. Jessica began spinning. She lost her balance. With a shriek, she fell to the floor and began to roll.

Finally, Max gave a good hard tug, and Jessica tumbled out — through the curtain and into the dark backstage.

Her head hurt. Her side was bruised. Her friends were giggling.

"Are you okay?" Selena asked.

"I'm not sure," Jessica replied.

"*Pssssssst . . . pssssst!*" a voice hissed from deep backstage.

Everyone fell silent.

There was nothing back there. Nothing Jessica could see, anyway. Just blackness, and the outline of one big box.

"Who's there?" she called out.

"*It's almost time for you to go to class!*"

The box. The voice was coming from the box!

"Yeeps!" said Quincy.

"*Yeeeeeeps!*" answered the box.

Quincy sprang back — but Jessica reached for the box and pulled it open. She grabbed on to something. She pulled.

Out popped Santa Claus. A big, stuffed Santa pillow with a sign on it that said PROPERTY OF REBUS ELEMENTARY SCHOOL WINTER FAIR.

Quincy cracked up.

Max was looking at Mr. Beamish in awe. Mr. Beamish had thrown his voice into the box. "Will you teach me to do that?"

Mr. Beamish just folded his arms and smiled.

8

The Big Show

Jessica looked out across the audience. It was hard to believe the school day was over already. This wasn't practice anymore. This was real.

The show had begun. And every eye was on her.

"Next, a trick with food!" she said, opening up a carton of eggs. She picked up one and smiled. "Hmmm . . . what would happen if I just threw this into the audience?"

"YEAAHHHH!" everyone shouted.

The show was working. It was really working! Even though Selena kept blushing and forgetting her lines. And Quincy flipped a whole deck of cards into the audience by mistake. And Wilbur Doodle kept hogging the stage.

It didn't matter. Magic was in the air.

Jessica relaxed her arm. "Naaahhh, too messy."

"YEEEEAAAAHHHH!" Everyone was laughing, stamping feet, cheering Jessica on.

"*You can't throw that in here, Jessie dear!*" shouted Wilbur Doodle. "*If you do, I'll make it disappear!*"

Jessica slowly smiled. She lifted the egg to her shoulder. She looked at Andrew

Flingus, who was way back in the last row of seats, asleep.

And she flung the egg out over the audience!

"Andrew, watch out!" someone shouted.

"Huh?" Andrew fell off his seat.

The trick had worked perfectly. The egg was still in her left hand. She held it tightly, making sure no one could see it. "Ta-da!" Jessica sang. "The egg has vanished!"

"Ow! Ow! It landed in my face!" shouted Andrew Flingus. He got up from his seat, covering his face and howling.

Max dropped Wilbur Doodle and ran to the edge of the stage.

Andrew ran to the stage, then turned around to face the audience. Grinning, he pulled his hand from his face. *"Hello. I am a dummy. I love my mummy. And this is Max. His ears have wax!"*

"Mr. Flingus!" Mr. McElroy said, walking toward the stage.

Andrew was gone in a flash.

"And now, the Floating Selena Trick!" Mr. Beamish announced. He and Quincy were carrying Selena onto the stage by her shoulders and feet. She was pretending to be asleep. A big blanket was draped over her, its edge sweeping along the floor.

Mr. Beamish gently lay her across a chair at center stage. Quincy lowered her feet onto another chair.

Then, after a moment, Selena started to rise. First her legs, then her body — up off the chairs!

She floated for a moment, and slowly settled back down, until she was on the chairs again.

Then she fell off.

Her fake legs went flying out of her

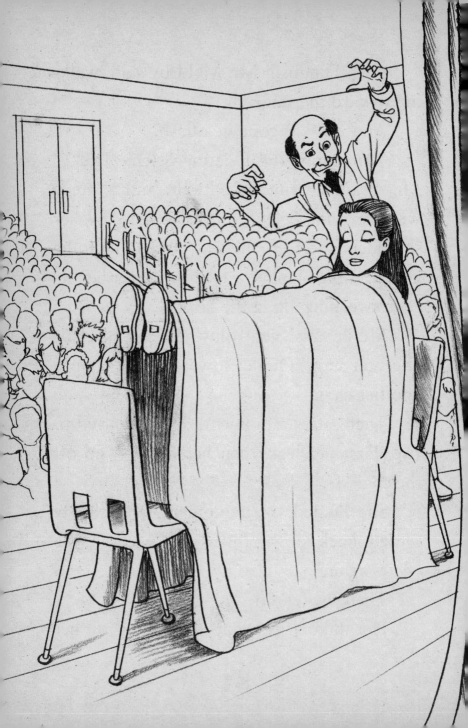

hands. Everyone could see how she'd done the trick — by sticking the fakes out of the blanket as she sat up on the chair!

Ruined, Jessica thought. *The show is ruined.*

But Selena calmly stood up, grabbed Wilbur Doodle, and said, "I think these belong to you."

She fitted the long, fake legs onto him. And then she danced him off the stage, to laughter and clapping.

The Disappearing Quincy Trick was last.

It started badly. Jessica and Quincy collided backstage. Max rolled Jessica up too fast. The blanket was so dusty, she couldn't stop coughing.

But it worked. Perfectly.

And at the end of the show, the whole school stood and stamped their feet.

"YEEE-HAAHHH!" shouted Mr. Beam-ish from backstage.

"They like us!" Max said as the four friends joined hands to take a bow. "They really like us!"

Jessica barely remembered the snacks they ate after the show. Or the big talk by Mr. Beamish, when he told them how proud he was. Or the cleanup, after Max managed to spill the entire carton of raw eggs on the floor.

Her head was in the clouds as she walked with Max, Selena, and Quincy into the hallway behind the stage.

"We're cool, we're cool, and we're the best club in school!" said Wilbur.

"You know, you're getting good at that voice-throwing," Jessica told Max.

"Guys?" Selena asked. "What happens if the whole school signs up for the club?"

"After our great show, even the teachers might sign up," Quincy said.

"One-eyed Pete, too!" Max said with a giggle.

"Uh-oh," Selena muttered. "You know, we still haven't figured out that mystery."

"Today's Friday," Max said. "He's supposed to appear — and get everyone!"

As they walked, their footsteps echoed in the empty hallway. They passed Mr. Flint's computer room, the prop room, the lighting room. They walked faster and faster.

As they turned the corner, they were practically jogging.

"*Myyaaaaaah . . . help me . . . HELLLP MEEEEE!*"

"Yeeps!" squeaked Quincy.

"There!" said Selena, pointing to the janitor's closet. "It's in there!"

Max walked in the opposite direction. "Bye-bye, I have homework."

"No you don't!" said Jessica, pulling him back.

She took Quincy's hand. Quincy took Selena's. Selena looked at Max's dirty fingernails and put her arm around his shoulder instead.

"We are the Abracadabra Club. We solve this mystery together," Jessica said, stepping toward the door. "We are not afraid."

"*MYAAAAAAAH!*" screamed the voice.

"Yes we are!" squeaked Max.

Jessica held the doorknob. Slowly she turned it and opened the door.

Crash!

Thump.

They all peered into the darkness. A bucket lay on its side. A few janitor's supplies had fallen from the shelves. An eye patch dangled from the ceiling. And a long black sash lay on top of a file cabinet.

But the room was empty.

One-eyed Pete had disappeared.

9

Fearsome Friday

"It *has* to be Andrew," said Selena as the Abracadabra Club walked home from school. "He's the only kid who would hide in a dark, stinky closet and not mind it."

The janitor's closet had a door in the back that led to the basement. Andrew could have made the sounds, using a paper-towel tube to make his voice sound deep and low. Then, waiting for the right moment, he could have escaped through the back door.

"There's only one problem," Jessica said. "You have to be smart to think of something like that."

Quincy read from his pad, "Okay, here's what we have so far. Three suspects: Andrew, Mr. Flint, and Mr. Beamish. Mr. Beamish can throw his voice. We have heard the ghost noises seven times. Well, five, really — not counting Andrew in the cafeteria and Mr. Flint in the computer room. I heard noises near the chess room, but that might have been Mr. Flint, too. Jessica heard moans and voices in the hallway and backstage. And Noah heard them at the after-school program."

"It couldn't have been Andrew at the after-school program," Selena said. "He always goes home right after school to eat."

"And when I heard the moan in the hall-way, Andrew was in class," Jessica said. "And so was Mr. Beamish."

"But Mr. Beamish can throw his voice," Max said.

"He couldn't have thrown the bumping and thumping we heard in the closet," Quincy pointed out. "Somebody was really in there."

Selena shook her head. "Cross Mr. Beamish off the list. He's too nice to do mean stuff like that — hiding in closets, sneaking into the after-school program."

"Good point," Quincy said, drawing a line through Mr. Beamish's name.

"Would Mr. Flint be mean enough to do that?" Jessica asked. "Who would want to make people so scared?"

No one said a thing.

All Jessica could think about was the patch-eyed pirate on the computer screen.

Jessica told her parents about the magic show at dinner. It took her until dessert time to finish the story.

"I wish I could have been there," said Mrs. Frimmel. "I bet you were a big star!"

"Not really," Noah said. "She stinks."

Their dad stood up to clear the table. "Now, you two have fun while we're gone. We rented you a movie —"

"Where are you going?" Noah asked.

"To the theater," Mrs. Frimmel said. "It's one of our last rehearsals for the play."

"No!" Noah cried out. "It's Friday. That's when One-eyed Pete comes!"

Mr. Frimmel chuckled. "It's Friiiiday," he said in a spooky voice. "I'll get them on Friiiiday!"

Noah covered his ears. "Don't say that!"

"It's only a line from the play, sweetie," their mom said.

Jessica put down her fork. "It is?"

Mr. Frimmel nodded. "There's this ghost in the play. An old pirate named Mortimer. He tries to haunt this little hotel run by three old sisters. Each week he tries to scare them, until finally, one Friday —"

"Ralph, please, we're late," said Jessica's mom.

"Tell me the rest!" Noah said, stomping his feet. "Don't go!"

"Wait!" Jessica cried out. Suddenly, everything was starting to make sense — the moaning, the sash, the eye patch. . . . But she needed to see something first. "Mom, Dad? Can I see a list of the actors?"

Mr. Frimmel looked at his watch. "Now?"

"Please!" Jessica said.

With a sigh, her mom gave her a sheet of paper from inside her shoulder bag. "You can keep it."

"Thanks!" Jessica said. Carefully, she looked down the list of names. And she saw exactly what she had expected to see.

Racing to the door, she put her hand on the knob. "Let us go with you. Noah and me. We'll watch the play. And Noah will see it's not as scary as he thinks."

Noah stopped crying.

Mr. and Mrs. Frimmel turned to each other.

"YEAAAH!" Noah cried, leaping to his feet. "Can I be in the play, too?"

Noah was such a ham.

"I'm going to call Quincy and Max and Selena!" Jessica shouted, running back through the living room. "They have to see this, too!"

10

The Ghostly Guest

Jessica, Noah, Quincy, Selena, and Max sat in the twelfth row of the Rebus Elementary School auditorium. Onstage, three women were acting the parts of the sisters who owned the haunted hotel. A younger woman stood nearby and kept yelling, "Louder!" She was dressed in black, and Jessica guessed she was the director.

"Will someone tell me what is going

on?" Quincy whispered to Jessica. "I was in the middle of this really fun extra-credit math workbook when you called!"

Selena's eyes were wide. "I love plays," she said. "I always cry at plays."

"This is a comedy," Max said.

"There's a ghost in the show," Noah whispered. "I read about it."

"You can't read," Jessica said.

"Can too!"

"*Sssshh!*" Selena shushed.

"But my dear ladies!" said a man onstage in a very loud voice. "I do believe there is a spirit in this hotel!"

"I told you!" said Noah excitedly.

"I'm not afraid," Max whispered, taking out his magic wand. "I learned a wizard spell that protects you from ghosts. *Abracadabra . . . fliplock!*" He scratched his chin. "Or is it *flaplick*?"

"Did anyone hear my question?" Quincy asked. "Why are we here?"

"Just watch!" Jessica said.

Clank ... clank ... clank ... came a noise from behind them.

"Ooooh, here comes the ghost!" Selena said softly.

Jessica felt Noah's fingers grabbing her arm. Selena sat forward. Quincy looked up from his work. Max held up his wand.

Slam! went a door.

Boom! went the sound of fake thunder. The lights flickered on and off.

"*MYAAAAAAAH!*" came a deep, loud cry through the theater speakers.

"Yeeps!" said Quincy.

"I want to go!" Noah screamed. He jumped out of his seat and began running up the aisle.

"Come back!" Jessica shouted.

Out of the darkness, at the back of the theater, a man had appeared. He wore a patch over one eye and a big black sash around his waist.

"IT IS FRIDAY!" he yelled. *"I WILL GET THEM ALL ON FRI —"*

Noah ran smack into him.

With a cry of alarm, the man stumbled backward. Noah fell to the floor.

"Cut!" shouted the director.

"Noah!" Jessica ran sideways through seats toward her brother.

Max was waving his wand frantically. "ABRACADABRA . . . FLEEBNOK! I mean, FLOOBNIK! Wait —"

Jessica ran up behind Noah. The director rushed up the aisle. Quincy tried to step over the seats but fell. Selena jumped over him.

The man knelt down. He reached for his

eye patch and pulled it off. "Are you all right, sonny?"

Even in the darkness, Jessica knew the voice.

"Mr. Skupa?" said Selena. "You — You're —"

"A bad, bad man!" said Noah, and he slapped him on the hand.

11

Pete Speaks Again

"Next stop, the Old Rebus Sweet Shop!" shouted Mr. Skupa. "The scoops are on Skupa!"

The rehearsal was over. Most of the cast members were cleaning up or putting on their coats. Soon everyone — the cast, Jessica, Noah, Quincy, Max, Selena, and their parents — would be heading out for ice cream.

Jessica and her friends waited in the hallway behind the stage. Noah was running back and forth, wearing Mr. Skupa's sash and trying to scare people.

"This place doesn't seem so scary now," Selena said. "Thanks to Jessica."

"She's a genius," Max said.

"Well," Quincy said, "I *was* about to figure it out myself, of course."

"I still don't understand how you got it, Jessica," Max said.

"It was because of that line — 'I'm going to get them on Friday!'" Jessica said. "Noah had heard the strange voice say it at school. But at dinner my dad said that it was a line from the play, too."

"And you knew that some teachers were in the cast," Quincy said, "so you figured that someone has been practicing his lines during school!"

"Wait," Max said, "it wasn't One-eyed Pete we've been hearing?"

"No, Max," Jessica replied. "Anyway, I made my dad give me the list of cast members. Sure enough, there were three teachers — and Mr. Skupa. I wasn't sure who was playing the ghost until we got here and watched rehearsal."

"So that was Mr. Skupa we heard in the closet today. He was practicing his lines," Quincy said, "but when we opened the door he was gone — into the basement to do his job."

"Okay, that makes sense," Selena said. "But what about that pirate on the computer screen, in Mr. Flint's room? And why did Mr. Flint sound so angry with Mr. Skupa?"

"Mr. Skupa had been looking up information for his costume," Jessica said. "He had accidentally left the computer on and Mr. Flint was angry."

Max scratched his head. "But I don't get it. Why would Mr. Skupa hide in closets and stuff?"

"Because he needed to practice his part. Normal people don't moan and groan in public!" Selena replied.

"*Myyaaaaaah!*" screamed Noah, pretending to bite Jessica's leg.

Jessica sighed. "You're so right, Selena."

At that moment, Mr. Skupa came rushing out of the auditorium. "Time to close up the school!" He switched to his ghost voice. "*I'm going to get some ice cream on Friday — myaaaah, and I'm taking everyone with me! Who wants to come?*"

"EEEEEE-HEEEEE-HEEEE! WAIT FOR ME!" screamed a voice behind Jessica.

"Yeeps!" said Quincy.

They spun around. But the hallway was empty.

"Who was *that*?" Selena asked.

"Not me," Noah said.

"Not me," added Quincy.

"Max — ?" Jessica said.

Max was already halfway to the door.

Even with his head turned, you could tell he was laughing.

The Abracadabra Files
Magic Trick #3
The Floating Dustpan

Ingredients:
One dustpan with a long stick handle
Two hands

How I did it:

1. With my right hand, I lifted the stick handle of the dustpan. IMPORTANT: I made sure the BACK of my hand was facing the people watching.
2. With my left hand, I grabbed my right wrist, just below the hand. It looked like I was helping to hold my arm up.
3. Secretly, I slipped my left index finger over the dustpan handle. I could then press the handle tightly against my right palm!
4. I uncurled the fingers in my right hand. Hidden from sight, my left index finger was still holding the dustpan against my palm. Mr. Skupa thought the dustpan was floating!

The Abracadabra Files
Magic Trick #4
Cutting Erica in Half

Ingredients:
Two ropes, each about six feet long
A small piece of thread
Stool or platform

How Jessica and Max did it:

1. The two ropes had already been tied together in the center with thin thread. When Jessica held up the ropes, her hand covered up the thread.
2. When Max and Jessica stretched out the ropes behind Erica, they were arranged like this, with the string holding them together:

A   B

3. Then they brought ends A and ends B together in front of Erica and tied a knot.
4. When they pulled, the string broke. It looked like the ropes had gone through Erica!

The Abracadabra Files

Magic Trick #5

Jessica's Vanishing-Egg Throw

Ingredients:
Jessica's arm
Egg (a small ball works, too)

How Jessica did it:

1. She lowered her hand across her body, as if she was getting ready to throw the egg.
2. She turned her head and *looked* to the spot where she was going to throw it. Really looked. That's the key. Everybody was looking where she was looking.
3. Because everyone was looking away from her, she could drop the egg into her other hand — and no one noticed!
4. When she "threw" the egg, her hand was empty!

The easiest trick in the world. But one of the best.

The Abracadabra Files
Magic Trick #6
Floating Selena

Ingredients:
2 Chairs
Long sheet
Two poles
Selena's shoes and socks
Masking tape

How Selena did it:

1. As she was carried onstage, her feet were actually on the floor. She had taped a sock (stuffed with cotton) and a shoe at the end of each pole! She made sure to hold them so it looked like her own feet were sticking out the end. The sheet covered her, and it draped all the way to the floor, so no one saw Selena's feet!
2. When Mr. Beamish and I lay her down on the chairs, Selena's real feet were still on the floor. She simply stood up, raising the fake legs, too.

Well, at least she *tried*.

About the Author

Peter Lerangis is the author of many different kinds of books for many ages, including *Watchers*, an award-winning science-fiction/mystery series; *Antarctica*, a two-book exploration adventure; and several hilarious novels for young readers, including *Spring Fever!*, *Spring Break*, *It Came from the Cafeteria*, and *Attack of the Killer Potatoes*. His recent movie adaptations include *The Sixth Sense* and *El Dorado*. He lives in New York City with his wife, Tina deVaron, and their two sons, Nick and Joe.